Withdrawing Fables From The Memory Bank

AleXander Hirka

Published by AleXander Hirka, 2024.

Table of Contents

With deepest gratitude to Tammy Remington — partner in life and art — for helping me to keep on keeping on.

• • •

Withdrawing Fables From The Memory Bank & Other New York City Reveries

• • •

First edition. 30 November 2024

• • •

Introduction • Withdrawing Fables From The Memory Bank •

Depositing Curious Fabricated Recollections
(in Six Chapters)

~

When it comes to the past, everyone writes fiction."
— Stephen King

~

The past is ever accumulating. Memories are just memories of memories. And looking back is yet one more rewrite.

I invite your imagination to override your skepticism and for a few moments indulge your credulity in accepting the fact that I took an actual time machine back to 1963, New York City, in January of 2024.

[Background: H. G. Wells, who had written about it eleven years earlier, brought the gizmo to the U.S. during his 1906 visit and gave it to Mark Twain.

Twain — who in the apocryphal work "War of The Words" hinted that both he and Wells were Freemasons — had the machine in Connecticut until his death four years later. J. Edgar Hoover, a known Mason, got his hands on it and used it to travel back to medieval times . The rumors about these travels ranged from him visiting Thomas Aquinas to discuss communism to his meeting with a wealthy cloth merchant, Thomas Paycocke, for procurement of fabrics related to a crossdressing fetish.

At around the time that H. G. Wells' image was included on the cover of the Beatles' Sgt. Pepper's Lonely Hearts Club Band album, a friend of mine, also a Mason (to-remain-anonymous), made me aware of the actual existence of such a time travel device. But it wasn't until I decided to write this piece, which was to take place in the late 1960s, that I hopped down to a certain Manhattan Grand Lodge and asked for an opportunity to use it.]

Once I was transported back to New York City I ended up staying with my friend Zĕna Kōan—who had taken the time machine back to this period a couple of years earlier. Since she was working on a novel about a homeless woman surviving the streets, she felt this was a good place to be. Having scored an apartment in the East Village, and a job at an Italian restaurant on 12th Street, she decided to stay there for the rest of the decade.

There was a small extra room in her apartment that had recently been vacated by a woman that Zĕna referred to, lovingly, as the "slum goddess of the Lower East Side." I was welcome to stay as long as I wished. And as it turned out — I stayed in that room for 6 years, through 1969.

In the relative shift of Time within fiction—utilizing the ten dimensions of string theory—nobody in the present time even noticed I was gone.

I was very grateful to have Father Time's assistance in having the six episodes I wrote there appear in print in the present over a four month period.

While there I did my hunt-and-peck typing on a brand-new model Olivetti typewriter, the Lettera 32, which a friend of Zĕna's had just sent all the way from Italy. (It was the same model that Francis Ford Coppola used to write the screenplay for the motion picture *The Godfather*. But that would be in 1972, a future unknown to all but us time travelers. In 1963 he was just working on his first film *Dementia 13*.)

I had grown up in New York City during those years so I understood some of what these young people were going through. While there, I was visited by ghosts of the past and spirits of the future—some who cajoled me to include them in these stories, and others who coaxed to be left out. All in all it was a productive period for me.

That era was filled with excitement. There was activism and voices raised in resistance to the prevailing political and social narratives. Experiments in the arts — literature, visual art, and music — were emerging. The dissent in the air carried a certain hope for change. I was glad to immerse myself in all of that again since it seemed to be painfully missing in my present.

It was there that I met my characters. I wrote down their stories — their struggles, their sorrows, and their joys. Let me introduce you to them now.

— Chapter One: The Penguins and Goof Gas

"Not Basil in Kindergarten"

The nuns. There was a murder of them, like crows, all black when seen from behind. With veiled pleated habits and veils, seemingly gliding along the hallways of St. George Ukrainian Catholic School, they appeared more bat-like. However, the white wimples surrounding their faces led to kids' whispers to classify them as penguins.

The priests, all called Father, were the source of authority. And the distributors of corporal punishment. A thick rubber ruler in these men's hands, coming down on a outstretched hand caused a burn that lasted into seeming eternity—especially if the crime, like passing notes in class, demanded two or three per hand.

•

No amount of rubbing spit into them afterwards ever seemed to sufficiently ease Basil's burning palms. And yet every time he was thus corrected for his misbehavior he applied this placebo to soothe the pain.

(Decades later he saw that very same rubber device, with the very same imprint he sworn he'd seen as it had descended towards his hand—The Discipliner™ ©—at a sex boutique.)

Basil was twelve years old, and lived with his mother, Maria, and fifteen year old brother, Marko, on Avenue C. Their father was missing in action during the war and not much was ever said about him.

Truth be known, Bohdan, Basil's father, had been with the Galicia Division during World War Two. This was an infantry division of the Waffen-SS, the military wing of the German Nazi Party, which was made up predominantly of volunteers with a Ukrainian ethnic background from the area of Galicia.

Connections with his few relatives had been lost across the ocean and so nobody knew about this — not Basil, nor his brother. Their uncle Tomas, who stayed in the Old World, never mentioned anything about this in his letters. Their mother was adapt at ducking anything related to the topic.

As you will come to see, being omniscient, I am informed about all kinds of lesser known things. Trust me.

•

Christina was in Basil's class at school.

Her mother, Tania, had arrived in New York in 1947. She met Josef, another recently arrived immigrant, on the Staten Island Ferry, and they were married the following year.

They wanted a good education for their only daughter, and so budgeted to send her to the local Catholic school—named after the dragon-slaying saint.

(Since Shakespeare's Henry V called for help from this very saint at the Battle of Harfleur, he was certainly an inspiring enough hero for the kids of the Lower East Side of New York City to venerate.)

As the events of that day obviously made an impression on Christina, her diary for Monday, 2 October 1961, makes note of her beginning friendship with Basil. They were in the same sixth grade and after one of the regular duck and cover air raid drills their eye-rolls and smiles met. Sister Theodosia made note but said nothing.

The day before, on the other side of the country, in Nevada, Operation Nougat—a series of 44 nuclear tests—was proceeding on schedule. A bomb named "Boomer" was detonated. Tourists, who had been flocking to Las Vegas to watch the explosions from their hotel rooms were disappointed—these newfangled underground testings didn't produce the nice clouds.

Basil and Christina sought each other out at lunchtime.

Perhaps in the interest of introducing cultural diversity to these children of Eastern European parents, the main course that day was chop suey—which they both enjoyed in spite of its clear glutinous sauce.

Individually they had both entertained thoughts regarding the absurdity of these bomb drills—as well as the daily standing with their hands over their hearts and looking at the flag for the Pledge of Allegiance—but they were also smart enough to keep these thoughts to themselves. Now they had someone to share them with. As the school year progressed and they were always around each other, their friends giggled and called them boyfriend and girlfriend.

•

During the following summer their families had different vacation plans and so they saw very little of each other around the neighborhood.

But sure enough next September, there they were, back in school, corralled by the nuns, crawling under their desks to protect themselves from nuclear bombs.

"Maybe all the adults have inhaled Goof Gas," suggested Christina at lunchtime, in response to their drill earlier that day.

"Yeah", replied Basil, "Looks like Boris Badenov and the Pottsylvanians have gotten to their brains."

Thus they signaled to each other that during that summer they had both seen a certain episode of the Rocky & Bullwinkle cartoon show.

In it, something called Goof Gas was deployed against the U.S. by the Boris Badenov character to render the most brilliant minds in the country utterly stupid.

In January Christina turns fourteen. Her diary mentions her getting a record player for her birthday. She starts spending her allowance buying 45rpm records. "Wipe Out" by the Surfaris. "Please Please Me" by The Beatles. "Puff, The Magic Dragon" by Peter, Paul and Mary. "It's My Party" by Lesley Gore.

Throughout the school year she and Basil remain close—this time around exchanging an extra batch of eye-rolls in March for the ritual of Ash Wednesday. As well as the collection tins — with an image of Jesus' agony at Gethsemane—that are supplied by the school to put coins in during Lent; later to be returned full to the school.

•

The summer of 1963 diary entries include shared trips to Coney Island. Basil's brother Marko, who is now almost seventeen, comes along with his girlfriend, Abby, who is approaching sixteen. A seagull swoops down and grabs a hotdog from his hand.

There is mention of holding hands, and a first kiss, with Basil.

Christina writes that the new school year has begun—and that the duck and cover drills have stopped. As every previous year, during Lent the Stations of the Cross are broadcast over the PA system, and all the classes follow along with the rosary.

She buys four 45rpms — "Blowin' In The Wind" by Bob Dylan, "Martian Hop" by the Ran-Dells, "Donna the Prima Donna" by Dion and "Washington Square" by The Village Stompers.

She writes of her and Basil's upcoming graduation at the end of the school year. Catholics, in response to the heathenism brewing in teenage bodies, have separate high schools for boys and girls. Christina ponders with growing sadness how their paths might diverge—as they in fact will, when her family moves to Philadelphia the following year, and his to Brooklyn.

There's an entry in the diary about a time in class when Basil got caught reading a paperback of Ian Fleming's "Doctor No".

Sister Theresa confiscates it, but returns it after class. She tells him — I'm glad to see you reading, but you can do better than this.

Christina's parents watch Bonanza, but she prefers the silliness of The Beverly Hillbillies. She and Basil both like the New York Yankees.

A nun comes into the classroom in tears — to announce that the president has been shot.

●

The following year, 9 February 1964, they are both sitting in front of their television sets watching the Ed Sullivan Show—separated by a few blocks—Basil on Avenue C, Christina on East 10th Street.

They are among the 73 million viewers who are about to share an extraordinary musical experience.

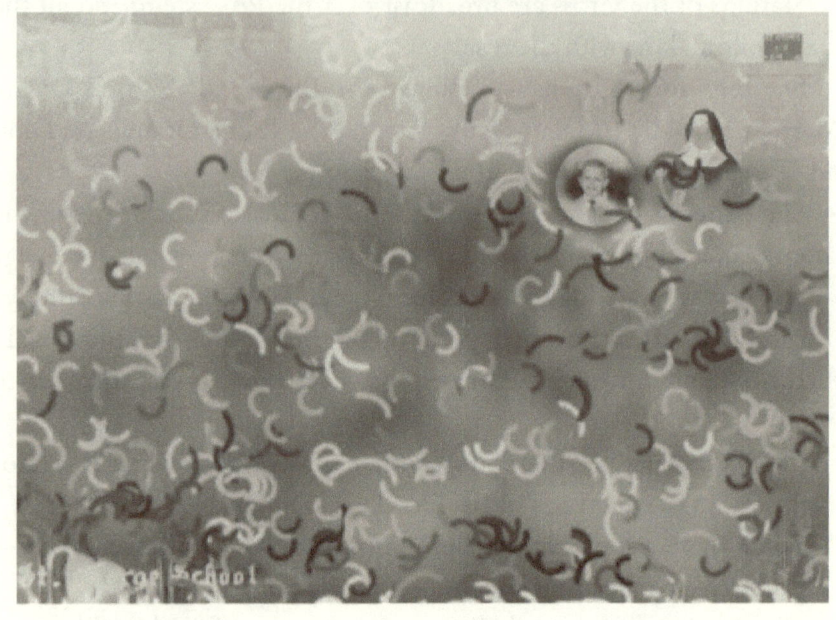

"Not Basil in 4th Grade"

• • •

— **Chapter Two: All The Rage**

"Graduation. Not Basil. Not Joey."

Our story opens on a Monday in November of 1964, with a view from up on top of one of the many construction cranes where the Lincoln Center for Performing Arts was rising. A twenty slipped to the worker on the crane got us this interesting overhead shot.

We see Basil, a fifteen-year-old high school freshman emerging from the subway station and walking towards Power Memorial Academy, the all-boys school he is attending. Basil's family, mother and older brother Marko, moved from the Lower East Side of Manhattan to Brooklyn during the summer—and this is his daily weekday commute. This morning, as he heads into the building, his thoughts are filled with concern for his brother.

•

Last year, when Marko was seventeen, just graduated from high school, he was hoping to get job with the post office. He did all the necessary preparations and a couple weeks after his eighteenth birthday he became a US Citizen.

The nightmare he had not considered came a month later in the form of a notice in the mail that he had to register for the Selective Service.

The United States has been in Vietnam since the 1940s, but their geopolitical empire strategies were expanding, and a fresh supply of young men was needed.

Marko and his girlfriend Abby have been together for a year. They met on the Lower East Side, where she still lives. Around Christmas of last year Abby dropped out of high school. She wanted to make money and move out. She got the working papers necessary to get a job at 16. Her mother supported her decision. Her father threw the Christmas tree across the room.

Marko and Abby catch time together wherever they can, often meeting for lunch as they both work in the Garment District. They have a friend who gladly offers them a spare room for occasional overnights—otherwise sexual rendezvous occur in hallways and on rooftops. Ask any New York City teenager how it goes.

A song that would have been a soundtrack to their love, "Wouldn't It Be Nice" by The Beach Boys, would not exist for another two years. "Under The Boardwalk" by The Drifters would have to do.

•

The corporal punishment that existed in grammar school continues here in high school—this time administered by the Christian Brothers of Ireland—but Basil's skills at avoiding the smack or whack have gotten much better.

He does get a note from the principal to give his parents because his hair is too long — yeah yeah yeah—and once for wearing a paisley necktie instead of the regulation dark and sans pattern.

He won't hear me anyway, so I can tell you that Basil had his first LSD experience this past summer.

•

This December afternoon there was "school assembly"—a pep rally.

Basil sat with Joey in the gymnasium bleachers. They met a couple of weeks ago—both taking track as a required "physical education" alternative to avoid team sports. Discovering they lived in the same Brooklyn neighborhood, soon they even commuted to and from school together.

A bit of patriotism, a sprinkling of religion, and then up stepped the school's basketball star, Lew Alcindor (later Kareem Abdul-Jabbar), for some praise and applause. The gym teacher followed with some treacly words to impress upon each youth that every one of them could become a superstar at whatever they chose to do. Just P&P—Persevere and Practice—and the house, two cars, Catholic wife and baptized kids will be yours.

Then the high school band stumbled like a drunk through a medley of Beach Boys songs. Basil and Joey shared eye-rolls.

As they left the assembly they both shook hands with the 7+ foot tall basketball star who was standing by the door—and on the subway home that day agreed how impressed they were with him.

Joey brought up the riots in Harlem and Bed-Stuy of the past summer.

Joey is black. One of his older brothers had brought a copy the Harlem Youth Action newspaper, in which Lew Alcindor had interviewed black citizens who were tired of segregated schools, dilapidated housing, employment discrimination and wanton police violence.

There was certainly no mention of any of that at the pep rally.

Keep your eye on the basketball—not, like the folk protest song says—on the prize.

As one year ends and another begins, come listen to the radio on top of the refrigerator at Basil's home. It's a posthumously released single by Sam Cooke — who was killed in December—promising that "A Change Is Gonna Come".

•

Over the following months both Basil and Joey became more involved politically, reading and going to protests together. The war overseas, and the racism here, fuel many of their conversations.

In March thousands of Marines are sent to Vietnam.

Without much conversation, or even words to really understand their feelings, Basil and Joey would occasionally stay overnight at each other's homes and began exploring sexually.

•

On a class trip to Washington DC all the students were lined up to shake hands with Robert Kennedy, the new senator from New York.

As ordained, hands were shaken; eyes were rolled.

The weekend before freshmen Basil and Joey graduated it is announced that The Beatles will be awarded the MBE (Member of the Most Excellent Order of the British Empire). Also, that American airplanes bombed a hospital for persons with leprosy in Vietnam, killing 140 patients.

While the band struggles with Elgar's Pomp and Circumstance March, the graduates walk up to the podium to receive their diplomas.

Both fans of Mark Twain, they signed each other's yearbook with a quote from the writer.

Joey in Basil's yearbook: "*Whenever you find yourself on the side of the majority, it is time to reform (or pause and reflect)*."

And Basil in Joey's: "*Man was made at the end of the week's work when God was tired*."

Look closely.

As orchestrated with details as some cinematic scene—calculated to establish a particular time and a place—the radio on top of the refrigerator finishes announcing that President Johnson was dramatically increasing the number of troops in Vietnam and doubling the number of men drafted from 17,000 to 35,000 per month.

The kitchen curtains are still, no breeze to balm the hot and humid July weather.

Just as "Like A Rolling Stone" by Bob Dylan begins playing, Marko arrives home with Abby — she with a black eye.

The slap from her father today was the turning point. They'd discussed their situations before and this pushed them to their decision—it was time to make the big changes.

Marko again confirms to his mother and Basil that there was no way he would cooperate with this war, that he was going to continue to refuse to register with the Selective Service. He and Abby were going to take the savings they had accumulated, research some possibilities, check in with friends of friends, and in the coming month they'd be moving to another city to live under the radar of both Uncle Sam and Abusive Father.

Maria, Marko's mother, gets in touch with a relative in Cleveland who offers the young couple a place to stay until they work out exactly how they are going to proceed. Hugs and tears followed.

"Eve of Destruction" by Barry McGuire was playing on the radio.

"Certificate of Graduation. Not Marko."

● ● ●

— Chapter Three: Old Clothes and Newspapers

"Next Stop, Bushwick, Brooklyn"

At first it comes from very far away, faint, somewhere near the horizon-edge of Basil's dream world. *Old clothes and newspapers.* The proclamation approaches, slowly, increasingly louder. *Old clothes and newspapers.* Along with a wooden cranking sound, the voice begins to fill his room. Old clothes and newspapers. He leaves sleep completely behind, lays there, listening, as the sounds pass and begin to diminish. *Old clothes and newspapers.*

It is like this every Saturday morning. He yawns, stretches his arms, gets up, and goes to the window—open to the warming weather outside. Old clothes and newspapers. The old man, like clockwork, pushing his wooden cart down the Brooklyn street, calling for offers to his weekly recycling parade. *Old clothes and newspapers.*

The Callery Pear trees outside his window are just beginning to bloom—their white blossoms are notoriously known—here's a brief dendrology lesson—to have a smell similar to semen.

Over breakfast Basil's mother, Maria, asks if he'd help her carry a package to the post office. This is the third parcel she has mailed to her older son Marko, who has been living in Cleveland with his girlfriend Abby, since they left New York in October of last year.

As she is seventeen, Abby's father — the one whose abuse she fled — has no legal control over her. But finding out that his daughter has left with a "draft-resisting hippie", he gives the FBI a call.

This action is added here to even further flesh out the distastefulness of this character in the story.

Marko's mother gets a phone call from the investigators. With Basil watching, she responds in a feisty tone, intended to discourage future calls, that she has *no fuckin' idea where her son has gone.* They share a smile.

•

The city is bristling with protests. 380,000 men were to be drafted into the military, more than double the previous year. The media reports on the evening news that thousands of U.S. soldiers are dying in Vietnam—30 percent of who are under 21 years of age. For future U.S. military adventures, the evening news would learn how to more efficiently omit and insert certain information to keep the citizens supporting the troops, no matter what they are being assigned to do.

The civil rights movement continues to grow and make strides all across the country. Women are organizing into a movement, and along with a growing rebellion from gay men, they are all boldly speaking out against the chronic discrimination they face.

Basil and his friends go to protests and spend a lot of time in the East Village, hanging around St. Marks Place, absorbing the growing energy of resistance and hopeful change.

·

A few blocks away, in the West Village, three gay men, inspired by the civil-rights *sit-ins*, protest by doing a *sip-in*—requesting a drink while proclaiming they are gay—at the Julius Bar. The ensuing legal actions will overturn the state law that had prevented businesses from serving homosexuals.

This newspaper has yellowed and is crumbling—so do handle it carefully—but look at this The New York Times article from that time: "Three Deviates Invite Exclusion by Bars". Consider it a nudge towards critical thinking and proper use of grammar when looking at your daily newspaper.

·

Marko and Abby live as anonymously as they can. He writes letters to his mother, through a cooperative friend's address, in case the mail is being checked. Based on the probability that this case doesn't warrant phone-tapping, he also occasionally makes calls from phone booths. This is how Abby finds out that her mother has moved out and is sharing an apartment with a friend in the Bronx. They begin a correspondence also.

The runaways manage to procure work at a Cleveland hotel that doesn't question their ages or credentials. Marko is a dishwasher at the hotel's Elbow Room restaurant, and Abby works in housekeeping.

They've made friends with a small group of people who called themselves hippies with whom they often get together, hanging out over pot luck dinners. The conversations circle around politics and sex and drugs and rock 'n' roll. This is where Marko and Abby first hear a record by the band called The Fugs, who reflected the cultural zeitgeist they were experiencing.

They've been quietly inquiring among their circle about the possibility of procuring an abortion.

•

It's the summer of over-the-top reactions to the Beatles-are-more-popular-than-Jesus controversy. In some Southern states, radio stations are organizing bonfires for Beatles records and memorabilia.

Meanwhile in New York, Basil is delighted in managing to get one of the rare "butcher cover" versions of their new album "Yesterday and Today", which had been withdrawn from circulation. When his mother is out, he and his friends smoke pot and flip the vinyl over and over on his new stereo.

Here's a polaroid someone took of them sitting in Washington Square Park, listening to Allen Ginsberg read his poetry under the trees.

One late afternoon, as the blistering August temperatures were slowly dropping—some pigeons on a rooftop at Knickerbocker and Covert cooing in relief—Basil walks by, hand-in-hand with his new friend Sarah, going towards the Ridgewood Theater on Myrtle Avenue.

Sarah, at nineteen, was the oldest in the circle of friends who were mostly seventeen. She was already a serious film fan, and was behind their choice to go see this new foreign film—called "The Face Of Another". Japanese, it was his first film with subtitles.

A couple weeks ago, along with their mutual friends Joey and Walter, they had walked this same way to see a retrospective showing of the 1946 film "Citizen Kane". Walking home they all raved about various aspects of the film.

•

Under pretenses that Abby has another job she quits her position at the hotel in the fall. She and Marko both think it best as she can no longer hide her showing belly.

Somewhat rudderless, young love pushes them on—along with fears of being parted, even jailed. They withdraw from their circle of friends. The letters home to their mothers make no mention of their dire situation.

•

While Bob Dylan sings — "Darkness at the break of noon / shadows even the silver spoon." — an environmental disaster strikes New York.

For a few days a nightmare smog of carbon monoxide, sulfur dioxide, smoke, and haze pervade the city and beyond.

People have been advised to stay indoors. Maria, Basil's mother, who has emphysema—probably from decades of chain-smoking—is having a hard time. But their Thanksgiving dinner, with Basil's friends dropping by and helping out, is still quite lovely.

Basil and his mother take turns briefly talking on the phone with Marko who says there is a lot going on but doesn't elaborate.

•

Look. In their small Cleveland apartment, the baby emerges in a bathtub with warm water. Abby and Marko, the mother and he her midwife, push through the situation. They have given the boy a name. Behold, Christopher.

•

New York City is blanketed with deep snow. The airport has been shut down.

The hospital provides Basil a cot so he can spend Christmas Eve with his mother. The nurse comes in and clicks on the television. It is the premiere of the "Yule Log"—a film loop of a burning log in a fireplace, with accompanying holiday music.

That's nice, his mother thanks the nurse, *but do turn off the sound—I really hate Christmas music.*

Even amidst this difficult situation, Basil smiles at his mother's delightfully cantankerous attitude.

"Somebody's Summer of 1966"

• • •

— Chapter Four: Secrets, Reliable and Unreliable

"Unreliable History"

In February Basil's mother's got news that her brother Tomas had passed away. He had stayed behind with their parents in what Maria always referred to as the *Old World*. Their parents—father Ukrainian, mother Polish—both died there over a decade ago.

As they were getting quite old, Maria did visit them once by herself when Basil was very small. It was the last time she saw Tomas.

Basil knew little about his Uncle Tomas except what his mother occasionally read to him from letters he sent. His uncle was a writer for a newspaper in Krakov. He didn't marry and had no interest in traveling to the United States. When he sent photos—there were a few under magnets on the refrigerator—they were of him and his three cats.

There is a book on Maria's self. A collection of short stories Tomas wrote in Polish. It was published a year before Maria took Basil, a toddler, and his older brother Marko and moved to the *New World*. She's often wondered when, or even if, she would ever mention it to Basil. A barrage of difficult questions would surely ensue, and, if she were to be honest, even more difficult answers.

•

While Basil was out with his friends she sat leafing through the book.

The title of the book, "Niewiarygodne Nenadiynyy", translated to the word "Unreliable"—twice—first in Polish and then Ukrainian, Tomas had written in Polish. He used *Lys Mykyta* as his middle and last pen name—which translates to Sly Fox in Ukrainian. Tomas Lys Mykyta, author.

The book was really a vanity project, a personal attempt to deconstruct the history around him in fictional form. Only a few dozen copies were ever published.

Tomas filled his story with such melodramatic scenarios, and exaggerated events, that it was hard to gauge how much was brought forth from his real life. Yes, he had situated them in the places and times they lived in, but Maria could see how almost each character was a composite of many people — becoming fictional through amalgamation.

To avoid them being pegged as any certain individual, Tomas had taken a great effort to blend and interchange identities, mix past and present, and have the characters do things they never would or could have done.

One section of the book — visiting the actions of an infantry division of the Waffen-SS, the military wing of the German Nazi Party, which was made up predominantly of volunteers with a Ukrainian ethnic background from the area of Galicia — was the cause of much consternation with his Ukrainian family. Denying that any of their family had been part of that infantry division, their critical reactions focused on a character they claimed represented Basil's father, Orest — who had died in the war when Basil was very young. Tomas' cousin Oksana angrily proclaimed that the book should be called "Bankrupt Memory Fables".

The narrator in Tomas' book was often breaking into the storytelling. Things sounded plausible enough — one would get a sense that this event must be true — but then again, maybe not. Unreliable as non-fiction, questionable as fiction

If Tomas's life had been an Orson Wells film, one of the final scenes may have been the disposing of his earthly possessions — with a copy Tristram Shandy by Laurence Sterne, a book whose fictional permutations had inspired him, being tossed into a fire.

Maria tucked the book back on the shelf and went to make herself some coffee

•

Basil sits in the kitchen writing a long letter to his brother Marko in Cleveland. He writes about the anti-war protests and the riots going on in Harlem and the Bronx. He sees Phil Ochs in concert in Central Park. He includes a photo a friend took of him playing stickball. "It's about the only game I've ever gotten good at," he notes on the back.

He writes about an incident at a neighborhood cemetery near where he and his friend were wandering, smoking a joint. They heard a high-pitched sound—was it a cat or a voice saying "mama"? When they reached the area where the sound was coming from there was nobody there—but the head of a little cherub from one of the tombstones had been broken off and was laying next to a flat stone in the ground, engraved Mama. "Quite spooked, we took off."

The radio on top of the refrigerator is playing a new version of the last year's hit "Wild Thing", parodying the voice of Senator Bobby Kennedy.

•

Christopher came into the world a few decades before Safe Haven laws allowed for the legal surrender of a newborn. Knowing they could not provide him with a home, Marko and Abby carry out their difficult decision — with a box and blanket, a safe hallway in the neighborhood, and an emergency phone call from a phone booth across the street—successfully. Only they know his name. Their hope is that someone will rename him with love.

They are silent with each other for days afterwards, an emotional smog making it hard for them both to breathe.

They will break up some months later, never to see each other again.

•

"Hey kid. I hear there's a big protest being planned for the Pentagon in a month. They want to exorcise the demons in that building. Much needed! Think you could possibly make it? I'm going to try.

And did you happen to see the Doors on Ed Sullivan last night? I read that they told Morrison to switch the lyrics from "Girl, we couldn't get much higher" to "couldn't get much better" and he defied them. Guess they won't be on that show again. This drug paranoia is crazy. Love, Marko."

(Postcard, postmarked 18 September 1967, Cleveland—received at Basil's mother's friend's address.)

•

Loads of buses were organized from Union Square to go to Washington, D.C.. for the March on the Pentagon. Basil's mother, Maria, has packed him a lunch and he sat with his back against the pedestal of the Abraham Lincoln statue, waiting for the buses to start loading. He was going to make this trip alone—his friend Phillip bailing at the last minute.

He made acquaintance with those sitting nearest him on the bus and the conversation was lively. The range of people was amazing — from young kids to seniors—all driven with a passion to stop the militarism.

In Wilmington, Delaware, the bus broke down and they were told that a replacement bus was being sent—but that they would have to wait at that spot until it arrived.

One passenger, a man in his 40s, with long black hair wearing a thick wool cape, mentioned in passing that the state of Delaware still used the whipping post. Basil expressed doubt—it couldn't possibly be! Hey, ask the next man-on-the-street, the man suggested.

And so Basil stopped a man walking by and asked if there were still public whippings in Delaware. The man looked Basil over, then the ragtag crew of protestors standing next to him, and replied "Yeah, but not enough of them!"

Basil sat down on a large *I Don't Give A Damn For Uncle Sam I Ain't Going To Vietnam* sign—lost in thought, feeling much older, maybe wiser, and far more afraid. He was going to be 18 years old soon—and the United States' military conscription numbers were in the hundreds of thousands.

The replacement bus arrived almost two hours later—getting to Washington too late for the initial rally with Phil Ochs, Norman Mailer, Noam Chomsky, Paul Goodman and many others.

Getting off the bus Basil joined the thousands marching towards the Pentagon where the proposed exorcism was to take place.

As they had planned, he was still hoping to connect with his brother Marko later, near the feet of Abraham Lincoln.

"The Whipping Post, Georgetown, Delaware"

• • •

— Chapter Five: Bang Bang

"Pro-war demonstrators and Anti-war protestors / My Lai Massacre Memorial, Quảng Ngãi province, Vietnam"

Dear Basil.

Thanks for writing.

Another six inches of snow here in Cleveland last night. Just like in New York it makes things quiet and beautiful for a couple days—but I'm ready for April showers and flowers next month.

The constant caution of living underground gets exhausting. And since things ended with Abby, being alone gets crazy-making sometimes. She seems to have left town. I'm glad you and I met last year, however briefly, so I could tell you about what has happened here. It's still hard to talk, or even think about it. Tortures me. I can only hope that things go well for all of us.

Oh yeah—a magazine piece I read recently about the Lincoln Memorial said that the shoe we met beside in Washington is a size 40. Big man.

Sure doesn't look good for this war to end, even with all the outrage and protests happening. The newspapers posted that great photo of a guy placing a carnation into the barrel of a soldier's rifle guarding the Pentagon, but I guess the levitation and exorcism of that monstrous place didn't quite do the trick. That power won't yield to flower power.

Hey—see if you can track down a short book at your library. It's called The War Racket, written by a Major General Smedley Butler. In 1935 he had thoroughly exposed what these Masters of War are always up to. Do check it out—it is really powerful. They should replace the Pledge of Allegiance in grammar schools with readings from it.

I have a friend, Charlie, who went over to Vietnam. He recently wrote from some area over there they call Pinkville. It was obvious he couldn't say much, but between the lines I could sense the horror of what is going on.

What the hell is this country doing?

Pisses me off that they can question you about your "relation to a Supreme Being" when applying for conscientious objector status. What are you thinking of doing?

Cheers, bro. Marko.

·

Pass the sugar, please.

I wonder how things are over at the school, he said. *It's been over a month already since the police moved in and removed the protesting students.*

Just then the radio in this coffeehouse near Columbia University begins playing Cher's "Bang Bang (My Baby Shot Me Down)".

When the song ends there's a news-break announcing that Andy Warhol had been shot by a woman at his downtown office.

Wow, that was a creepy musical segue, she said. *I wonder if the announcer knew what song he was following.*

Pretty twisted, he replied. *If you wrote that into a short story your readers wouldn't buy it. But hey, equality—now it's not just men with guns.*

The radio continues—mentioning that tomorrow would be two months since Martin Luther King was shot

Seems to be a theme this year. My friend goes to South Carolina State College. In February some state troopers fired on demonstrators and killed three. At this rate even college campuses might not be safe.

"Hey Joe" by Jimi Hendrix comes on the radio.

(Their conversation would come back to both of them a couple days later when they hear about Robert Kennedy getting shot.)

•

Hi Marko—

I'm just sitting here with mom getting ready to watch Ed Sullivan in a little while. Jefferson Airplane are supposed to be on. Thought I'd get another note out to you.

The whole world was indeed watching Chicago last month. Including us here in Brooklyn. Really frightening.

We were glad to get your note that you were indeed safe and back in Cleveland —and that you didn't get maced or arrested. I was there with you in spirit.

Things seem more insane than usual in the world.

Whether we get Nixon or "Happy Warrior" Humphrey in November we're guaranteed more bloodshed. I saw George Wallace question "the judgment of persons who march in the streets" and added an "honorable peace in Vietnam" (beware of that word honorable)—to his racism.

I'm guessing that Pat Paulsen couldn't do a worse job—but I guess we've not yet reached the point when television clowns or Hollywood actors can get elected president. It is obviously just a question of time.

Love, Basil

•

•

Abby's Nightmare.

She's holding a little girl, her daughter, up to the window so she can see the pigeons that have landed on the sill.

A beam of light enters the room through the window. It is coming from a 1950s movie flying saucer hovering above the church across the street.

She sets her daughter down who begins to fade in front of her. Seconds later she sees her running up the beam towards the ship. It takes off with her.

For a second her thoughts turn towards her firstborn, Christopher, in Cleveland.

But at that moment a hole opens up in the ceiling and through it she sees her upstairs neighbor, sitting at a typewriter, looking down at her. There's a small Christmas tree next to him.

I heard you two arguing like hell last night, he says. *I wrote it all down.*

He tosses a sheet of paper and it flutters down in front of her feet. As it lands on the floor a dagger comes out of nowhere and pins it to the floor.

The hole in the ceiling seals up just as there are four knocks on the door — like the opening notes of Beethoven's 5th Symphony.

Startled, she asks *Who is it?*

The door opens on its own. It appears to be one of the aliens. He approaches her.

Take that off, dear, she says. *You'll scare the baby. Stop. Don't! The guy upstairs heard your threats last night. He wrote it down.* She points at the paper stuck into the floor.

And then it happens — chaotic, violent, brutal, murderous — inescapable.

There is overwhelming pain.

(In the past, waking suddenly from a dream, she would occasionally have a pain in some part of her body. She would wonder if the pain was psychological, cause by some aspect of the dream — or did she have some pain in her body that her mind created a dream around.)

She struggled upward trying to wake up. Now she was back by the window.

Her daughter is standing next to her with a terrified look on her face.

But then there was no pain.

The spaceship was back above the church. There was that beam of light.

It will be impossible for her to have any memory of any of it.

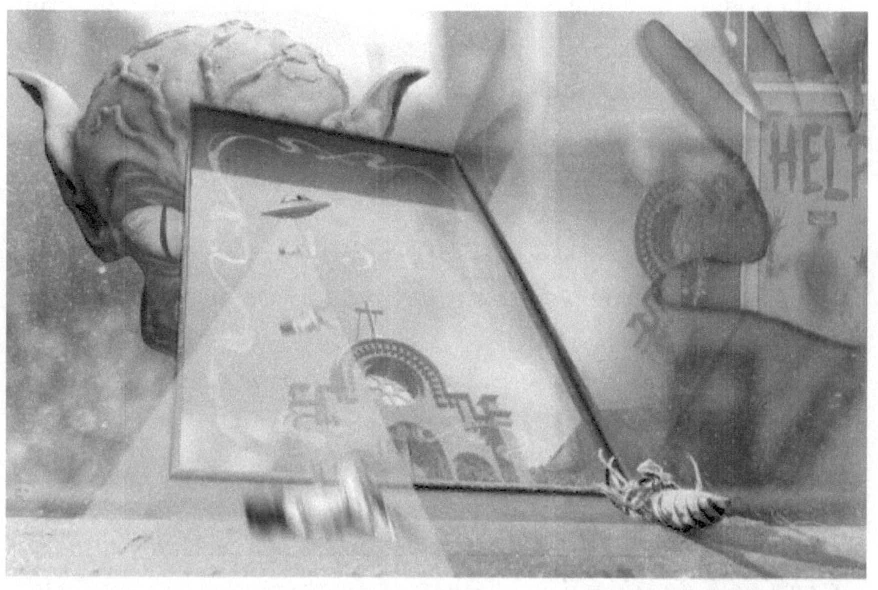

"Abby's Nightmare"

•

Basil's friend Sarah had gone off to college in Vermont, and ended up getting an apartment and living there. They had kept in touch and so when she was going to be visiting her parents in Brooklyn for the Christmas holidays, she reached out to get together.

They decided to go to the movies. The film playing nearby that night at the Ridgewood Theater on Myrtle Avenue, where they had seen a number of films together when she lived in Brooklyn, was "Night of the Living Dead".

Here they are sharing popcorn and watching a British Pathé newsreel of events for the year. Amidst the brief clips about the assassinations, the protests in Berlin and Paris, space explorations, European Cup soccer, and the election of Nixon there is a minute or so focused on a pro-Vietnam War march in New York City in May.

Thousands marching down 5th Avenue in support of the war. Flags. Men in uniform. Flags. Ladies along the route waving and applauding. Stars and stripes. Black and Vietnamese marchers. Signs—"Communism is the Enemy", "Draft Queers", "Support Our Boys". Children in uniforms having fun. Stars and stripes.

Overheard on their walk home.

• *That was a truly spooky film—low budget terror.*

~ *I'm glad we saw it together. The racial perspective at the end was interesting.*

• *Very true. I do know I won't be wanting to visit any cemeteries for a while.*

~ *Y'know, As we're walking here, and my mind wanders to what we've seen tonight, the one image that has stayed with me was actually something from that newsreel. The pro-war guy with his wife and kids, pushing a baby carriage, with American flags attached to it, with the little tot asleep in it.*

• *Yeah. That's the spookiest!*

• • •

— **Chapter Six: We Are Stardust**

"Last Year Of The Decade"

Radio announcer:

"This year promises to be a wild ride, folks.

In just a couple weeks in Washington, DC, Richard Nixon will be inaugurated the 37th president of these here United States.

And wow, if things go as planned, then by the summer it looks like humans will be leaving their footprints on the moon.

Meanwhile, in local news, this morning, across the river in Newark, police confiscated 30,000 copies of the new John Lennon and Yoko Ono album, entitled 'Two Virgins', which features a nude photo of the couple on the cover, for violating New Jersey's pornography laws.

And now—back to music—still holding the number one slot to start this year, Marvin Gaye with 'I Heard It Through the Grapevine.'"

New York City population had reached almost 8 million.

Stop and consider for a moment the estimate of 200 million sperm that compete for one human egg, and you will begin to see each of these 8 million as the winners of a very rare cosmic lottery.

And since every atom of calcium in their bones, oxygen in their lungs, iron in their blood, and carbon in their muscles, was made inside a star before the Earth was born—they are each and every one. . . *stardust!*

In February a severe nor'easter blizzard turned millions into *snow covered stardust.*

•

Spring.

During her visit to New York at the end of last year something reignited between Sarah and Basil. They had dated a couple years ago, but with her going off to college in Vermont the connection was mostly maintained through written correspondence.

She visits again briefly during spring break. They go see "2001: A Space Odyssey" at the Ridgewood Theater before she heads back. A conversation begins on the possibility of Basil moving to Vermont to join her.

Another conversation, one they've had many times, is about his ongoing intimate friend-with-benefits relationship with his friend Joey. Sarah has been understanding, supportive. *"I'm sorry you will lose that. I suspect you'll find a similar buddy up in the Green Mountain State. And Joey will always be welcome to visit."*

•

Summer approaches.

On a 23 inch color TV set up in one corner—mostly there for baseball games—the customers at the Lys Mykyta Bar on Second Avenue in the East Village, are watching the premier of the Johnny Cash Show. Special guest Bob Dylan is singing "Living The Blues".

•

Summer arrives.

A week after the solstice, in the West Village, New York's Finest raid the Stonewall Inn, the only "gay bar" in New York where dancing is legally permitted. Despite payoffs from the Mafia owners, the police occasionally made a show of raiding gay bars.

There were always some men, and a few women, who stood to be arrested for "cross-dressing" under the "three articles rule"—not having three pieces of gender-appropriate attire.

For several days afterward hundreds of patrons protest against police, demanding decriminalization of homosexuality.

•

Midsummer.

Hey Marko.

I was at Gem Spa this afternoon getting an egg cream and I glanced through a Farmer's Almanac. It declared that today was something called Lammas Day—the midpoint day between the summer and autumn solstices.

Enclosed is the poster for an amazing event coming up—sorry I had to fold it.

I got three tickets at the record store yesterday. My friend Tom from the Bronx is going and that other ticket has your name on it! All you gotta do is find a way to get here. Weekend of August 15. They're talking Creedence, Hendrix, Janis Joplin, Jefferson Airplane, The Who . . .

I'll be giving you a call later today and tell you all about it all anyway. Just wanted you to have this for inspiration to make it.

Basil

•

August.

Marko meets Basil in Monticello—and because the traffic is completely stopped in all directions, cars pulled off to the side of the road—they walk the ten miles towards Bethel, New York, to Max Yasgur's farm, where the concert event is happening. Shelves in the little stores along the way are already completely emptied. Richie Havens is performing as they arrive.

The next afternoon, under overcast skies, Country Joe sings —

"Yeah, c'mon on all you big strong men / Uncle Sam needs your help again

he's got himself in a terrible jam / way down yonder in Vietnam

so put down your books and pick up a gun / we're gonna have a whole lot of fun..."

Reveling in the music, sitting under the intermittent rain, shivering at night (arriving unprepared), tripping on mescaline, getting covered in mud, being fed by the Hog Farm commune, the two brothers shared one of the most amazing weekends of their lives.

In a New York City hotel room, watching the news on television, Joni Mitchell is converting her deprivation of not being able to make it to the event into a song.

"We are stardust / Billion year old carbon

We are golden / Caught in the devil's bargain

And we've got to get ourselves / back to the garden."

Afterwards, Marko makes his way back to Cleveland. Basil first mentions his thoughts about moving to Vermont.

•

Autumn.

Radio announcer:

"Thank you Ella Fitzgerald and Louis Armstrong for that fabulous rendition of 'Autumn in New York' on this last Autumn Equinox of the 1960s.

Here's a glance at the news headlines. Congratulations Willie Mays who on Friday hit his 600th home run, catching up with Babe Ruth.

The whole world will be watching as tomorrow begins the trial of the political activists referred to as the Chicago Eight, on conspiracy charges resulting from the riots at the Democratic National Convention last year.

On a lighter note—rumors are flying that recently engaged performer Tiny Tim will be marrying his bride Miss Vicki on the Johnny Carson show later this year.

Makes perfect sense for wrapping up a bizarre year."

There are four of them lounging around the room, smoking hash, and taking turns every 25 minutes getting up and flipping over the new Beatles record album "Abbey Road"—over and over—for hours.

Last winter these same friends were in this same room, taking turns flipping sides on the new Pearls Before Swine album "Balaklava".

Next year they would part ways — one to Vietnam, one to heroin, one to Jesus, and one to Vermont.

•

15 October.

By now more than 40,000 young men from the United States had been killed in Vietnam. On a regular workday Wednesday hundreds of thousands take part in the Moratorium to End the War in Vietnam demonstrations. A month later even larger events will take place.

President Nixon responds that the "silent majority" do not agree with the protests.

•

Postcard.

Dear Basil.

Just saw an article in today's newspaper. By a reporter named Seymour Hersh. He states that a Lieutenant Calley's men deliberately murdered at least 109 Vietnamese civilians during a search-and-destroy mission in March of last year. The shocker for me was that this happened in a Viet Cong stronghold known as 'Pinkville.'

Do you remember me telling you about my friend Charlie who was over there? Pinkville was the name he used for where he was stationed. He's missing in action. The lunatics have taken over the asylum.

Marko

PS Have you heard the new track by Frank Zappa called "Peaches En Regalia"?

It's dazzling! '

●

1 December 1969.

The Selective Service draft lottery is conducted. Days of the year are printed on pieces of paper, placed in opaque plastic capsules, and spun in a tumbler.

Lady Luck and Beelzebub preside.

Marko's birthday, 22 Jan 1946, is drawn as number 337 of 365.

Deciding he can be more valuable working to end the war while not living underground he registers—the late registry charges are dropped.

At a street protest months later he will burn his draft card. "I wouldn't go kill for peace no matter what."

Basil, born 3 November 1949, also has Lady Luck on his side, number 348.

●

Winter.

Marko moves back to New York, staying with his mother and Basil until he can settle himself in the city. Basil meanwhile is making plans to move to Vermont the following year.

Their mother, Maria has been spending time with a man named William, a likely candidate for the eventual empty nest.

•

Scene.

At McSorleys Ale House, Marko sits reminiscing with his old friend Ivan. They hadn't kept in touch but ran into each other recently and made a date to catch up. There is a light rain outside.

They talk over the times they spent together at St. George Ukrainian Catholic School—which is visible across the street through the windows of the bar. Memories of the harsh discipline by the priests and nuns now seem amusing.

"In retrospect I somewhat appreciate the education those penguins beat into us." says Marko, smiling.

"Listen . . . Marko. . . You mentioned when we ran into each other that you had lost contact with Abbey in Cleveland. I'm guessing your family doesn't know either, that they hadn't heard what happened, or they would have told you. It was really big news. She'd moved back here, married, so her last name was different. It happened like a mile north of here. I didn't want to get into the story when we met on the street, but I brought you this clipping from last year's newspaper which I thought you should see.

Marko reads the tabloid version of Abby's Nightmare.

As if he were suddenly deaf, all the sounds of the bar grow mute—a roaring silence. A dizziness follows—the framed pictures on the wall blur, smeared colors spin around him.

The lights dim.

Curtain.

•

•

The end of the year.

Marko's Dream.

It's nighttime. He's left McSorley's, walks past the Cube sculpture at Astor Place and down the stairs to catch the number 6 train.

The doors to the train slam closed just as he arrives. He sees a young man looking at him through the window in the subway door. The man smiles. The train leaves the station.

He sits on a bench. The face of the smiling man keeps coming back to him.

Then he's struggling up the stairs and out into the street, running from corner to corner — he wants to call somebody — but on every public telephone he comes across the rotary dial is unmovable, as if glued in place.

Out of breath now, his steps heavy, he's slouching towards the beacon of the Empire State building — thoughts locked in a groove, like a needle on a record album — repeating: Something about that face reminds him of her. Someday Christopher might look like that young man. Christopher might look like that young man someday. Christopher . . .

And then he's awake. On the L train heading back to Brooklyn. He had walked to 14th Street to catch it after leaving McSorley's. Must have had a few too many beers. He vaguely recalls some young man's smile. Looking at him through a window. Where was that? A smile so much like Abby's. Where did that image come from?

This will have to remain enough to hold him. He'll propose to himself that it was snapshot glimpse into Christopher's future.

He'll use it as a bandage of hope to wrap around the spikes of distress and anxiety that will emerge and rage over the years.

Until, maybe someday somehow, before Marko returns to stardust, a young man with a familiar smile will come knocking at his door.

"We Are Stardust"

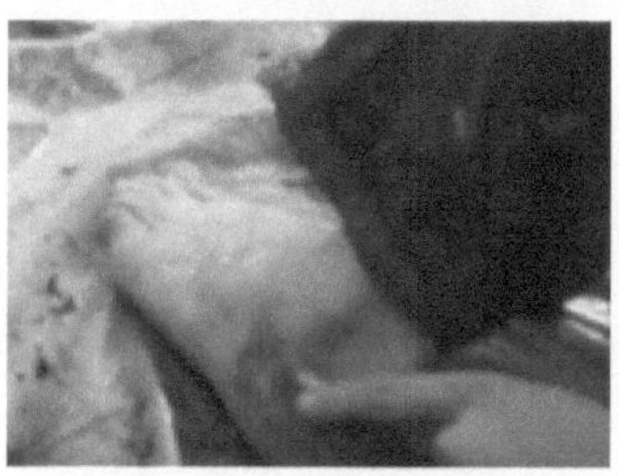

Author's note: I did attend the Woodstock celebration, but, being as they are fictional characters, I never met Marko, or Basil. However, amidst his few fading snapshots from the event, Basil does have this photo of his friend Tom scraping mud off his foot at the event.

• • •

Addendum • Other New York City Reveries •

.

.

.

"Because philosophy arises from awe, a philosopher is bound in his way to be a lover of myths and poetic fables. Poets and philosophers are alike in being big with wonder." – Thomas Aquinas

.

.

.

• From A Pillow In Harlem – Restless Horizontal •

"Sleepless Night"

He lays his head on the pillow, eyes closing to the outlines of the room created by the streetlight through the curtains.

And so his ears took over the vigilance. As his body relaxed on the bed, he pulled a cool smooth sheet over himself.

They had made love. She was half way to dreams already. Even during a war people need sleep, need touch.

Through the window from outside that familiar hum — something he'd never taken the time to identify, something just always there filling the night air. He has surmised a generator. He has imagined a hovering flying saucer.

But tonight, as happens so often these days, his thoughts bypass that industrial soundtrack and his mind is swept up by the waves, the convulsions—the horrible sickness that the city is undergoing—out there.

He often has a brief surge of restlessness after sex, an urge for flighty talk, but he doesn't want to wake her, and so the jumpiness takes a grip of him and pulls him out the window, drone flying over Manhattan—some attempt to grasp it all from overhead—to somehow hold it close before he can consider falling asleep. Desperate.

Desperate as parts of entire days have felt. Desperate out of fear, desperate for hope.

He has been out for brief walks and has seen first-hand the springtime bacchanal of trees and plants flowering. He has also sensed the silently pulsing anxiety that was blossoming everywhere.

He follows a siren howl towards where the hospital is—then over the dark rectangle of the park and downtown to where a convention center has been converted to a hospital—to take care of the city's overrun of sick. The streets are empty—an occasional cab, someone walking a dog. The bright lights of ambulances going up and down, left and right, like some characters in a video game.

He exhales a deep sigh and for a couple seconds is back in bed.

Just a short while ago he had been lost in amazing body closeness, flaring passions, the cosmic joining of two animals — he had managed to let go of time and place and they had dipped into eternity.

He inhales and now is back over Times Square—looking down at that amazing Abandonment seen in all the photographs that have been broadcast around the world—that archetype example of the sheltering tribes, tourism and consumerism strangled.

He finds himself on foot, walking through the Village and across that most beautiful bridge to Brooklyn—then on a Ferry heading out to Staten Island, Liberty's torch visible in the foggy harbor. Then other streets and neighborhoods he's walked a thousand times—Wall Street and Madison Avenue and Broadway, Chinatown and Loisaida and Hell's Kitchen, Joe's Pizza and Carnegie Hall and The Apollo.

And it just rolls in from different perspectives—at one moment from above, the next his feet are on pavement: Parkchester and the Botanical Gardens in the Bronx—Bedford-Stuyvesant and Coney Island in Brooklyn—Far Rockaway and Jackson Heights in Queens.

And everywhere he goes the streets are empty—he can't seem to conjure even one pedestrian.

He's had problems falling asleep lately. A pandemic can do that. A political two-ring circus can do that. He's exhausted from staying awake through the nightmares of the day, yet too wound up to relax into the ones of the night.

And how to to grasp this hallucination—this distortion of the place he loved?

How to encapsulate it?

If he could only capture it, contain it in a narrative that he could turn into a strategy. Something to go forward with, something to help with letting go of the fear. How can he embrace this?

Another siren on the nearby street pulls him back inside and into bed.

He lays there for an eternal moment—pondering the choice of getting up and writing down his scramble of thoughts, or just keeping on traveling around the city until he falls asleep.

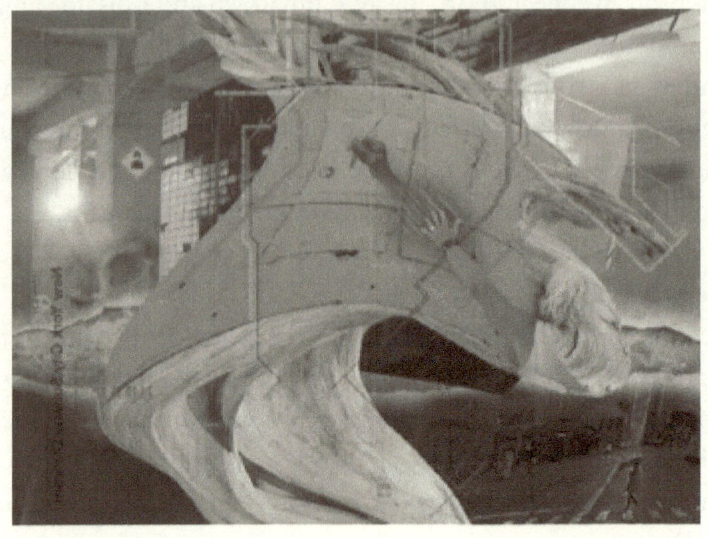

"Nigh Trip"

• • •

New Linoleum - Stand Back and Admire

•

"Traffic On Sparkle Boulevard"

On Avenue C,
on the Lower East Side,
sometime in the late 1950s —
new linoleum arrived
with fanfare and excitement.
Father spread out
the ocean of newness,
flooding the kitchen floor.

•

Visiting Uncle Sasha

who fashioned himself a poet
proclaimed with excitement, that —
anyone from the truly rich,
to the absurdly wealthy,
might never experience the joy
of this kind of renewal —
A *Grand Rejuvenation* he called it.
He said he'd write about it.

·

He extrapolated.
Primarily—
for those with never-ending spondulix,
nothing was ever allowed to get
that old, so food-stained, cracking
and curling in the corners.
What old things do they have
that could be
so dramatically replaced?

·

Aunt Sonia scoffed —
Like you would know!
This neighborhood has no such
unfortunates
as of which you speak.
Your fantasies of the rich
are all from that idiot box
you stare at every chance you get.

·

Visiting friends noticed
the shine right away—
stood back—appraised and praised—

Such luster, reflection.

·

But weeks later it was just the floor again.
and talk began
of a new opportunity for glory —
replacing the curtains.

·

Aunt Sonia pulled Uncle aside
You'll give us all names —
and think that this will give this scenario you've written credence.
But it never happened just thus —
this assemblage
of madeleine crumbs,
of lost time.
And I expect, she added,
you thought I wouldn't tell them.
Well, I will.

·

Yes, you just did, he finished.

"Memories have no colors, not even black and white." — Zĕna Kōan

• • •

• Stations of The Dross —Tales From Underground •

"Where It Stops Nobody Knows"

A screeching of brakes comes across the station.

"Please stand clear of the closing doors."

That dull thump of rubber as the subway doors slap shut may as well be the click of the ball dropping onto the numbers on the roulette wheel.
Your money is down so might as well relax into it. A winner? A loser? Look left, then right.
There's a chance that Lady Luck may even have a seat waiting for you.

Or else she's busy breathing on somebody else's dice—and you get dealt some warning sight, or stinging stench, that instead sends your mind on a strategy for preparing to bolt to the very next car at the following stop.

For starters today an average hand of high and low cards has been layed out in front of you. Nearest the door a woman reads a magazine, the man next to her with a small thick paperback, embossed cover—absorbed in a page turning world of suspense, military espionage, far from this mundane subway ride.

Announcement: *"If you see a suspicious package or activity, do not keep it to yourself. Tell a police officer or an MTA employee. Remain ALERT and have a safe day."*

Consult your Book of Odds and Chances on *today's* scenario:

Two teens are sharing music from a smartphone, one earplug each. And on either side of them, like bookends, sit two people who are both running their fingers along small print in black books. One has gold gilded pages. Holy Scriptures. Time traversing communiqués from different gods — one speaking to the bearded man dressed all in midnight black, the another to the Latina woman in partly-sunny-sky colors—blue and grey.

They're prospecting for inspiring thoughts—messages from the Creator-of-All-This.

All this?

This subway?

No — this train, as the books they read from, is very much human made.

They would both agree that *their* Author is the one who made the sun that is burning above ground right now—and yes, less reluctantly, the One who gave that man further down the car the withered leg he needs the cane to walk with.

That cane: human made. Wood for cane: Creator.

Cane in French is *une canne.* That is what those three travelers who just got on would call it—it is their language. But they do not notice the man with the cane—as they huddle over a subway map, trying to figure out some destination.

And what is the French for *do-rag*? — the cloth that the black man has covering his head. From his ears, where black wires end, even amidst the roar of the subway, you can hear treble tzzzzls emanating in a steady rhythm. His eyes are closed, his hands doings slight gestures to the beats. The woman sitting next to him, with similar wire attachments plugged into her head, sips some exotic sugar and water elixir from a plastic cup. Her tapping foot indicates that there is indeed music flowing from some source in her green bag; upward into her ears.

> *"Ladies and gentlemen, a crowded subway is no excuse for inappropriate sexual conduct. If you feel you have been the victim of a crime, notify a police officer or an MTA employee. Remain alert and have a safe day."*

At the next station a bit of the Caribbean enters via the sounds of a steel pan drum being played on the platform.

Music is a human creation of the most amazing kind. Some even think there are secret chords that please the Creator.

Transcending time and space, from every culture on the planet, the range of motivations to make music is endless — dance, joy, beauty, relaxation, sadness, defiance, escape—sometimes just making money.

The canned varieties, radio hits dropping down from shopping emporium speakers, are very limited by the mass market—that very human made game of control and distribution.

The rumble rattle soundtrack of the stampeding train doesn't seem to distract the young man who is reading a photocopied script of a play— closing eyes intermittently as he tries to memorize lines.

A woman reads her NooKindle electronic-pad-book thing— only glancing up for a second every time the recording blares —

"Watch the closing doors, please." Bing.

Without a book cover it's harder to judge the reader by their book.

And truth be told, every creature's up-and-down-scan-judgments are de rigueur on these underground rides ~ human measurements, analyses, and subjectively processed final categorizations of co-travelers.

We creatures do that — the constant silent buzz of brains using *what was,* checking *what is,* and riding headlong *into what will be.*

"The New York City Police Department would like to remind you that backpacks and other large containers are subject to random search by the police. Thanks for riding with us."

Another spin on the roulette wheel, another click of the ball—another stop. They get on, look left, then right—and briefly at you. There must be a precipitation prediction in the air as among the group to enter are two with umbrellas.

Stuck here for more minutes than expected, the man in the suit, for some internalized audience, displays the universal sign of exasperation: sliding his hands down his face while sighing loudly. His visage grows into visible aggravation as a Mariachi guitar duo enter the car at the far end and are making their happy way towards us.

The child whose fingers were skating madly on the surface of some electronic toy, stops and stares — first at the musicians' passionate strumming coming down the aisle, maneuvering around extended feet — then at the man struggling to lift himself up onto his wooden cane, reaching desperately for one of the poles to complete the process.

The others dodge their eyes as soon as the man's struggle begins, they don't want to see it—but out of the corner of their being they can feel it, feel the pain, want to keep it from intruding into their journey, their day.

One of the scripture readers watches, lost in thought, perhaps trying to ascribe a story of why a Creator gave this creature such a pain component. That analysis would certainly be a parable — one of endurance, acceptance, the rewards of an after-life — and perhaps a castigation on humans always wanting too much.

"If you see an elderly, pregnant, or handicapped person near you, please offer your seat. You'll be standing up for what's right. Courtesy is contagious and it begins with you."

The sombreros and guitars have moved onto the next car, and the old man now crosses the station platform, slowly towards the express train that has arrived. Doors open, doors close.

The roulette ball clicks into the next notch. More cards are dealt. New faces enter. Some bet on hope, others on resignation. The latter know the odds. Getting where you're going without major incident is as close to jackpot as can be expected.

"Please stand clear of the closing doors."

As the train nudges forward, spies, gods, music, and advertisements regain the attention of the riders. Some passengers close their eyes, others press buttons on various small screens. Heads full of ideas and plans ready to move down the tracks.

The wheel is slowly set back into motion. Red. Black. Red. Black.

Your stop is next.

illustration by T. Remington

• • •

• Back Yard Sunshine: Heliocentric XVI •

"Backyard In Harlem"

The orange tabby cat had two homes, one on the second floor and one on the third, up two separate fire escapes. Depending on the weather and the hosts' availability, there were always food and water dishes provided, often indoors through left-open windows.

The tenants knew of the arrangement — had even yelled an agreement across that space that his name was Sunshine (to which he seemed to respond) — but they had never met before yesterday. The shared yard between the two buildings, mostly just overgrown with weeds, was the cat's domain — occasionally challenged by other felines passing through and most often by a quite feral-looking cloudy grey tomcat.

Last night a battle raged somewhere in the yard. From one of the apartments up high a potful of water sailed down on the combatants. Followed by a particularly howling meow. Followed by silence.

The next morning both windows were open and the two tenants were looking down at the still orange body in the yard with some blood near its neck, and then back up at each other.

Later they put Sunshine's body, cushioned with fabric, into a boot box. Since they didn't own the yard property they waited until after sunset to return clandestinely.

Under apartment window lights and the moon overhead they dug a deep hole and buried him over two agreements: that Sunshine had a good independent life in this jungle between two sanctuaries—and that they'd get together for coffee sometime soon.

• • •

• COVID-33 — A Love Letter from Intensive Care •

"Keep Cool, But Care"

This email was sent to me a couple days ago, on 22 December 2033, by a nurse named Sylvie. It, and its attachment, are reprinted with permission.

"Briefly about myself. I'm a nurse at Bellevue Hospital in New York City.

This is my second time around with a coronavirus pandemic. I was a student nurse during COVID-19. I was exposed to so much devastating pain and death during that time, 2020/21—when over 2 million people died around the world. We were so unprepared and the struggle was so difficult—but with luck I survived; and am all the stronger for it.

Now we are on the very edge of 2034 and faced with a similar biological cataclysm.

Again, those of us who are on the front lines are doing all we can. Luckily this time around things should not be as devastating because we as a nation, and the world altogether, were so much better prepared to respond to a pandemic this time.

I am of course so very grateful that in my lifetime—towards the end of 2020— this country began its dramatic shift regarding healthcare and the government's sense of responsibility to all its citizens—when Bernard Sanders was elected president, god rest his soul.

I am sharing the following message with permission of the recipient. The sender was an 83 year old man who came into the hospital three weeks ago and whose health was steadily failing."

•

"Dearest ＿＿＿＿＿,

We've talked about it, we've cried about it. We did it before it got to this, and even over the phone a few times during these past weeks.

At our age you gotta—or it sneaks up on you. And surprises like this are unacceptable.

And yet—a surprise it will always be—no matter what, no matter when.

And so—I'm gone—not just the hypothetical we bounced back and forth—but like for real .

I'm typing this amidst daily decreasing energy. I'm making sure you'll get it when I go out that door with the EXIT sign and we won't get a chance to talk anymore.

Getting in a last word again. :-)

We've gone over all these thoughts many times so this is just a string-on-finger reminder.

You always bragged your great grandmother made it to a hundred and five. And your grandfather to a hundred. So your seventy-five year old DNA is that of a spring chicken.

Twenty five years was a hell of a good run for us, and I'm hoping you've got that many still coming. Without too much major pain—but we know how that is.

I accept your often gifted title to me, love-of-your-life, with the deepest gratitude. And I do think and hope you've got at least one more good love—okay maybe just a number two or three in the hierarchy of your life—but some human to share a rollercoaster seat on this Life thing—until it comes to a stop and it's your time to get off. Maybe we'll be done with pandemics for a while so it can be easier.

Damn you have so much love to give—and it better not get wasted! And not just on a cat, and god forbid on some dog.

These past three weeks, with fluorescents overhead, and sick people all around, have been difficult. One wants to either recover or depart quickly. The sense of panic has been minimal and the loving care quite amazing—so glad the one in 2020 didn't get me. But quite honestly, when they try to serve me up some Hope along with my lemon Jello they both taste completely artificial.

Thank you for following up to make sure they turned off that television over my bed. Daytime TV just fueled my misanthropic perspective of the species, and I did not wish to leave the planet in that state of mind.

Sorry to leave you the mess.

As we've gone over it: clothes to Goodwill, ashes in Central Park and lots of black trash bags for most of the rest.

Lovelust, ______________

•

"Since he felt he could trust me with the note he emailed to me, to pass along to his partner when the time came, she in turn has entrusted me to hold onto a copy. In fact she also gave me permission to share it with you, and if you wanted, to share with your readers. I have purposely deleted names where they appeared.
Back to the battle raging,
Sylvie."

———————

I hope you find this email I am sharing here somehow helpful as you face the dangerous world outside with your loved ones.

Stay safe. Remember to keep your distance and wash your hands.

And as the writer Thomas Pynchon said: "Love with your mouth shut, help without breaking your ass or publicizing it: keep cool, but care."

~ •*• ~

About the Author

Putting words to paper for fifty+ years, AleXander Hirka's fiction, poetry and essays often share methods he developed over decades as a montage artist working in graphic, video and audio formats. Assembling, juxtaposing or superimposing, and reshaping diverse elements, all in the service of creating a unified composition — a brand new whole, not fractured, but in its own logic a glimpse into another world.